You Are Not *Invisible*

Cynthia Milone and
Eagles Rise Up Student Leaders

ISBN: 978-1-4834-9678-8 (sc)
ISBN: 978-1-4834-9677-1 (e)

Lulu Publishing Services rev. date: 02/5/2019

Contents

Dedication Page

This humble work is dedicated to all those who felt invisible. A special tribute to my son, Sam, who has served as our inspiration to write this book.

America is suffering from a "bullying epidemic." Bullying finds its way everywhere; in playgrounds and in the hallways, at the bus stops and on the bus rides home, and sadly even online in the privacy of one's home. No one deserves to be bullied! No one signs up to be bullied. Yet, there it is, all around us. Left unchecked, bullying has a way of destroying schools, communities, and the lives of the children who deserve a bully-free environment to grow, to learn, to thrive, and to achieve. The students, staff, faculty, and Administration at Lake Zurich Middle School South have made it their mission to stomp out bullying and create the school and community environment that every child deserves. The LZMSS school-community is relentless in this mission.

Four years ago, Lake Zurich Middle School South introduced an anti-bullying blog initiative. The *Eagles Rise Up Blog* forum provided students with a safe place to ask questions and post comments about the insidiousness of bullying; *those they witnessed and those that were all too personal.* The blog provides the link "*See Something, Say Something*" where students can report a serious incident directly to the building Principal.

Student leaders, as well as their Club sponsor – 7th grade teacher Cynthia Milone – have kicked off the anti-bullying program each year since. The program's focus is on the incoming sixth grade students during the month of September. Throughout the program, students learn about the nuances of bullying and the devastating toll it takes on the victims and bystanders. By sharing her son's story about his experience as a victim of online bullying, Mrs. Milone let's students know they are not alone. She and the Club leaders make a personal appeal to students to stand up and be heard; *and defeat bullying.* She has tasked the student leaders with finding a safe place where all students could have a voice and never feel invisible.

Since the blog has been published, LZMSS has witnessed unprecedented, and incredibly heartwarming, changes. Students are kinder to each other. They are speaking up with greater frequency. They are more self-aware of how their actions impact others, and they are now talking more honestly and openly. The kindness of the students did not stay idle inside the walls of LZMSS. Soon, children thousands of miles away would become beneficiaries to this spirit of kindness that was being nurtured throughout the school.

In their quest to spread kindness, the student leaders held an all-school drive to donate nearly 6,000 pairs of shoes to an orphanage in Ghana. Through the generosity of LZMSS, orphans in Ghana were able to look up while they were walking. The doors to education, once shut because of their lack of footwear, were now open to them. Seeing the orphan' smile when the shoes arrived in the village in Ghana was an experience the LZMSS students will not soon forget.

Still not satisfied that their mission was complete, The *Eagles Rise Up* leaders embarked upon a new challenge. From this challenge, a book was born. Every chapter penned by LZMSS student author. Every graphic inspired by a LZMSS artist. Each inspiring story, picture, and poem tells the reader about the possibility for change, faith, hope, and of better times ahead. *You Are Not Invisible* has fictional stories written through the lens of the bully, the bystander, or the victim. Through the inspiration of each story, those who contributed hope that soon the bystander becomes the up-stander, the victim transforms into the victor, and a bully matures into a protector and a promoter. *Change* is the answer; *Kindness* is the catalyst.

The mission and vision to serve does not end after the last page has been turned. The mission to inspire continues thanks to the generosity of the Club leaders who have selflessly and lovingly agreed to donate all proceeds from the book to the Anthony Rizzo Foundation. The mission of the Foundation is to raise money for cancer research and to provide support for children and their families battling cancer. Through the support we receive, we remind those fighting the cancer that they too are not alone, they too are *Not Invisible*.

Chapter One

Bully's Perspective and Letters to a Bully

Dear Bully,

We are all equal and we are all different, I don't know why you want everyone to be the same. We all have flaws including you, you are not much cooler than anyone else, and no matter what you do you will always get a consequence whether it is good or bad. Also, it doesn't have to be from others. Living with the guilt could be your consequence. Words can never be erased or taken back, speak carefully. How would you like it if a kid comes up to you and says you look weird! How would you like it if someone talked behind your back? You can't "undo" your actions, what you can do is think about what you are doing and think smart. Think through all that fog that caused you to be a bully; think about your body language because every second you live. Personally Body language says everything about the person because it is the hardest to hide because sometimes you do it unconsciously and you don't even know that you did it. That's what hurts the most.

By: Luciya Kojenova

Dear Bully,

Yes that's what you are. It may not seem like it, but your actions have hurt someone. Have you ever considered that you could end up giving a person the excuse to take their own life? Do you realize that a person can die, because of you?

Some say that bullies have pent up aggression or a troubled past or are insecure, but if that is true, then this is an issue that needs resolving, not aggression. Most people aren't just mean to be mean, so what's your reason? All of your victims probably want to know.

I'm sure you have heard about teen suicide. It's quite common. But maybe you have not heard of the reasons behind it. A great percentage of teens commit suicide due to bullying. Do you really want to add to that percentage? Maybe take a minute to evaluate your actions.

By: Hannah Pratt

Dear Bully,

I'm not going to make this seem like something you wouldn't want to read, because I want you to read the whole thing. What I wanted to tell you is that you should be ashamed of your actions. You may not know it yet, but what you are doing is not ok. Being mean to someone may make you feel better, but if you understand what's happening to the person you're bullying, then you wouldn't feel so great. Let me ask you this. If you came to school one day only to find that people were constantly being mean to you, blackmailing you, or even doing bad things to you physically how would you feel? Would you feel like you were a great person? Would you feel only temporarily sad? Or would you feel scared to come to school because you knew that people were just going to be mean and that everyone was turned against you? Think about it.

By: Natalie Czarnik

Dear Bully,

Many people choose to bully their peers, and many of those people are only worried about themselves. Bullies are people that are not ok with themselves, so they point out the flaws of others. This is extremely unfair to the victims, and I think that even you, the bully deserve the chance to fix the harm that you've done. In years, maybe many, maybe few, you will realize how destructive you have been in people's lives. You owe to yourself to ignore your urge to hurt others, and build them back up instead. You probably have other friends that help you ruin lives that keep your inner voice blocked out. These are not good friends. Good friends want to help others, and don't want to hurt them. Every bully needs to realize this, I'm helping you do it sooner. I promise that you are digging a hole for yourself. Nothing good will ever come of what you are doing. Eventually, your brain will kick in and notice the harm you do. It will be much easier to bounce back from if you start now. There is a good chance you won't listen to what I am saying, but I strongly hope that you do.

By: Kayla Mesin

Dear Bully,

I'm sorry. I'm sorry that you feel the need to take your insecurities out on other people. I'm sorry that you feel that your only way out is to be mean. I'm sorry that you feel pain. I want you to know, I understand. Sometimes you feel like your life is terrible, so you don't want anyone else to be happy. However, do know, there are other ways to be happy. Try it. Do something nice for someone else. They might react weirdly at first, but you will probably feel proud. Even if it is just a little bit of happiness that you feel. Each time you do something nice the better you will feel about yourself. I know this is not easy thing to do. The more you practice good deeds, the easier it will get. It is also good to practice self-control. Practice not lashing out as soon as someone annoys you. Know that there are others out there like you. You are not alone! I hope this letter helped. Now I have one last message for you:

Be someone who you would be proud of!

By: Louisa Hagen

Dreams

A short story by Andrew Dziubinski

CHAPTER ONE

I sit on my bed, and I wonder about what I could've done to stop it. Should I have taken the weapon with me? Should I have treated them differently? What could I have done to prevent it? My mind is swirling around mixed thoughts of anger and revenge, when I realize I couldn't do anything to stop it, no matter what I thought. They were gone, and there was no way to deny it. I couldn't be seen like this, as a mess that would be mocked for the next 10 years. A male sixteen year old crying in public? That is a death sentence for my dignity. There was no way that I could go to school tomorrow in this condition.

I needed to find a way to hide the pain.

I lower myself into my bed, closing my eyes, and I drift into the world of dreams. As I arise in the clouds, I can make out a distinct figure out in the distance. "Ashton!" I scream, but nothing seems to come out. I try calling for Ashton again. "Ashton, do you hear me?" Nothing comes out once more. It feels as if I have an invisible piece of duct tape around my mouth. *How can he not hear me?* I close my eyes, and try to figure out what is happening. I open them again, but now there are two people out in the distance. The second one looks like a normal teenager, maybe a freshman in high school. He takes two steps towards Ashton, and looks down. Ashton is shorter than the freshman, about two heads down. They both glare over, and I catch their eyes. They both twitch, and start walking towards me. Their movements are unsettling, their arms and legs jerking back and forth. As I look closer, I can see the freshman wiping his eye. He looks as if he had just finished bawling his eyes out, but he wasn't crying normal tears. He was crying blood. The blood droplets had stained his white tank top and yellow shorts, along with his cheeks. The two kids were nearly next to me before they stopped. A good couple of feet in front of me, Ashton looks up at me for the first time. I notice he doesn't seem to have normal eyes. One eye was twitching uncontrollably, while the other was blankly looking ahead. It didn't seem like he had a soul behind them. The two turn their bodies and look away, with me now facing their backs. "Um… are you guys okay?" I said, in a quiet tone. Surprisingly, I had been able to speak. This was very bad in my case as I was about to learn. The two both snap their necks around in one swift movement, with a loud cracking noise breaking the silence in the clouds. They turned their heads slightly to meet my gaze. I am petrified, and beyond words. They open their mouths, and start cranking their jaws past the possible human limits. Now with their jaws fully open to where the back of their head are touching their spine, they start to vibrate. Loud, deep vibrations pierce through my eardrums. The lifeless puppets are getting louder and louder, and I try to cover up my ears, but alas, I cannot. From the throats of the two kids emerge two vile creatures. With blood red skin and putrid and overpowering smells, they slowly climb up to the opening of the mouth. The two finally step out of the still bodies of my brother and the teenager, but don't leave behind a spotless environment. My brother has holes throughout his neck, blood seeping from his veins to the floor. The freshman has his jaw still fully unhinged, looking like a baby sparrow getting his feeding from his mother. My eyes are wider than they have ever been, and they start to water from the rancid smell of stomach acid and blood. I start to feel my own mouth crank open, and I hear a snapping noise below my ear. The pain is great, but I can't move or cry or scream. I'm stuck in a nearly endless cycle of trying to scream and trying to tell myself to wake up.

Wake up.

Wake Up.

I jolt up in my bed, in a cold sweat. I try to remember the moments of the dream in my head over and over again. My eyes tear up, and I start to cry. I can't handle this by myself. I need someone to talk to. But who could I talk to? My mom? That's out of the equation. Ashton? No, he's asleep and doesn't want to deal with my complaining. My dad? Wait, where is my dad? I don't think I heard him come home earlier.

CRASH!

I jump up in my bed, frightened by the loud noise. What was that? My mind can't think straight after the wild dream, but I decide to get up and see if I can find where the sound had come from. I quietly sneak around the hallway of the house. The corridor feels endless, and it feels like I am being watched. The demons from inside my head keep screaming at me, telling me to keep going and follow my gut instinct. I should know never to thrust my inner voices, but I had believed them. I felt as if they were the only ones that were on my team. As I make my way down the stairs, the creeks and cracks only add to my anxiety. Do I really want to do this? I sigh, and I start to head back up the stairs.

CRASH!

The noise appears out of nowhere again, and I jump out of my skin. I rush down to the bottom of the stairs, and dash into the TV room. It's empty, but I hear some moaning in the kitchen. I tiptoe my way over to the kitchen door, and slowly open it. I see my father lying on the floor, with six empty cans of beer. I look over onto the wall, and I see two dark purple splotches upon the wall with shattered glass on the floor beneath it. I pick up a small piece of glass with a word on it. It reads Shiraz. I look up, and my dad is leaning up onto the refrigerator. My dad is a raging alcoholic. His New Year's resolution was to only go drinking once a week, and only have one glass of whatever he chose. I'm glad to say that the resolution lasted a solid nine days until broken today. He seems really wasted, and I can't say I'm surprised. He's reached over a point three on the blood alcohol content scales more than once, and he never could control his urge. He should've known better than to make his resolution something he couldn't keep to save his life. I take a glimpse outside, and I notice his car isn't outside.

"Dad, where's the car?"

He looks up at me with his bloodshot eyes and blinks slowly.

"Dad, where is the car?"

He mumbles something inaudible, kind of like a gurgling sound. Had it finally got to him? I've been praying at night, praying and wishing that the alcoholism would kill the scumbag after all these years. Still staring at me, in a drunken tone, he says the worst thing to say to me.

"Shouldn't you be in bed, Kyle?"

I am furious.

"Who do you think you are, telling me what to do? I came down here to check if everything was alright, and I see this filthy old loser lying down in a puddle of beer halfway to death's door!"

Dad scrunches his nose, and slowly straightened himself out. I can see the rage in his eyes, the inferno burning through his pupils. He clenches his fists and wipes his mustache. He speaks a single word, and I suddenly feel fear flowing through my body.

"What?"

I start to back away slowly to the door of the kitchen from where I came in, and he's there before me. I laugh nervously, the sweat seeping out of every pore, all at once. "N-Nothing, Dad. I hope you s-sleep w-well." I try to move past him, but he grabs my collar and slams me into the door before I can even touch the handle. He swiftly pulls my hair and slams my head repeatedly into the door frame, and I start to see stars. He yanks me off of the door, and I am flung onto the floor. He then lifts up his leg and stomps on my chest over and over. I can feel my rib cage snapping after every movement, and I can't breathe. I am starting to black out, but I'm able to wheeze out one more sentence.

"Dad...please...you're hurting me."

My dad stops stomping on my chest, and he steps backwards away from my limp body. I can see his eyes start to tear up, and he turns his back on me. I hear several sniffles, and I can guess that he was crying. He turns back around to look me in the eye, and continues to cry, but louder. What, is he feeling bad for me now? After I've already been beaten until I was black and blue? What an idiot. This was exactly how every drunk beating ended with my father. I'd say something that would hurt his feelings, he would nearly kill me with his own bare hands, and then he'd cry, usually followed by him passing out again. I guess I was supposed to feel bad for him, but how could I? It's not like he would change his ways for his own child. I should've learned after the fifth beating that I should no longer go downstairs to check on things when I hear a noise, but I just couldn't learn. I wouldn't learn.

I'd never learn.

Chapter Two

"You know, being your little brother actually sucks. I honestly can't even go to school without being trampled by your high school friends. Why can't you just tell them to back off?"

I sigh. Ashton believes that I control all of the high school students. How could I?

"No, Ashton. It's impossible for me to control everyone."

"You're big. You're tough. Can't you just shove people out of the way?"

"That's against my philosophy."

"What philosophy?"

"I don't hurt people. I wouldn't even hurt a fly."

"Well I think..."

"Oh my god Ashton, why are you so talkative today? Did someone tell you to talk so much you'd make my ears bleed?"

"Well maybe you should know how to make people's ears bleed, after all of your dumbness."

I stared off into the clouds, trying to figure out what he meant by that.

"That didn't make any sense," I remark.

I walk into the school, and walk over to my locker. Like usual, the hallway is packed full of seniors running into freshman, furious teachers outraged by the noise, and the small couples that always need to find a way to just stand by their lockers and kiss. This is my life. I put in my passcode to my locker, and I unlock it to find a small purple slip glide down onto the floor. I pick it up, and I notice it's a detention slip. Great, another detention. I look closer at it, and the reason sounds like something I've never done in my life. I got a detention for "throwing a cup of coffee in a teachers face." I've gotten detentions for not doing homework assignments and just messing around in class, but I couldn't believe what I was reading. This must have been a mistake.

I look around to see if anyone was watching, and when the coast was clear, I threw the small piece of paper in the recycling bin. I glance at my watch, and it reads ten minutes to seven. Crap! Class starts in two minutes! I slam my locker with great force and start sprinting towards my woodworking class. As I round the corner, I collide with someone way taller than me. Papers are flying everywhere, and I blink twice before I realize who it is.

"What are you doing, Mr. Strong? You could've killed me!"

"I-I'm sorry Principal Haddins, I was just..."

"There is no need for you to be running in the halls."

He then pulls out another detention slip and signs his name on it. He hands it to me, then stands up and storms off. Wonderful, I have a two hour detention to go to after school. Just what I need. I hear the loud chime of the school bell go off, and I remember why I was running. I jump up and continue barreling down the long hallway, and I finally burst through the doors of the woodworking classroom. The smell of gasoline and sawdust hits me like a truck. I look up to the board, and I don't see the teacher. With a sigh of relief, I sit down in my assigned seat. With my classmates all talking at once and slugging each other in the arm, I don't think they would've noticed I came in late. My best group of friends are hanging out by the power tools like normal. They are really the only reason I come to school, as they let me forget about the beatings and horrible things that happen in my life at home. I get up to go and talk to them.

"Hey guys."

They all look up at me, but don't say a word. They look back down again at something I can't see, as they were in a circle formation. I look at Rob, my old classmate from elementary school, but his eyes stay fixated on the small object in the center of the group. I repeat myself, but louder this time.

"Hey guys?"

They still ignore me, and I'm getting a bit aggravated.

"Hey, are you guys ignoring me or something?"

Rob looks up at me, and the next sentence he utters from his mouth changed my life forever.

"Go away. You're no longer our friend."

I stand there in shock, wondering if this is some cruel joke played for a couple of laughs at my expense. I was waiting for someone to start laughing and punching me in the arm. I was waiting for someone to burst out of the cabinet and yell "It's just a prank!" But it never happened. I was holding back tears, and I looked at Rob again. I wanted to reach out to him and ask him if this whole thing was one big joke.

I wanted to die.

I sit at lunch, stirring my soup with my spoon. I'm all alone at my lunch table, separated from all other classmates. This used to be the table where I would have food fights and where my friends and I would talk about girls. But it felt like a ghost town. I'm replaying the morning as I stare out the window of the cafeteria. Who am I? Do I need friends to be happy? What is wrong with me? I'm asking myself these questions right before I get interrupted.

"What's that on your face?"

A freshman points at me, and I don't understand. I look at him, puzzled.

"You, in the yellow shirt."

I look down. He is talking to me.

"What's what?"

"What's wrong with your eye?"

I suddenly remember last night, the fight my father and I had. Had he given me a black eye?

"It's all purple and stuff. That's disgusting, you should have that covered up."

I stand up.

"You shouldn't be so quick to judge, you don't know how I got this black eye."

"What, did your dad hit you a little too hard?"

I freeze. The words that had come out of the kid's mouth had ripped through my soul in a matter of seconds. I've been teased and pushed around year after year, and this was the last straw. I clench my fist, and I feel the anger coursing through my veins. I lift up my arm, and I throw a solid punch into the kid's nose. I heard something crunch. He stumbles backwards, and then falls limp onto the ground. He seems to pass out for a couple of seconds, but then slowly rises up. He touches his nose slightly, and blood comes pouring out, drenching his clothes.

"Ouch! My nose, my nose! I think it's broken!"

I look at my knuckles. I have blood on them, but it wasn't mine. I couldn't believe what I just did, I socked a kid directly in the nose. It felt dangerous. It felt wrong. But it mainly felt...

Good.

Ashton was right once again. I'm big and tough, so why should I have to be bossed around? I have the muscles to nearly cripple a fourteen year old, so what's the point of not using that power? I realized that I shouldn't have to bend to everyone's will. This was a new era in my life. I look down at the freshman.

"You'd better get going."

I've never seen a teenager run so fast before in my life.

CHAPTER THREE

"What are you in for today, Strong? Mr. Haddins wants you to meet him outside at 3:15, by the basketball court."

I sigh. I'm in detention for running in the halls, but I don't really feel like telling the school secretary about it. Like I said before, I've only gotten in trouble with my friends, but this is the first time I've gotten in trouble all by myself. I looked over to the back of the small room. There was nobody else in detention today, so I would be all by myself.

I sit down into a slumped position in the nearest desk, and look around to see an area only consisting of the desks and myself. The secretary knocks on the door. I jump, not being prepared for the knocking noise. She tells me she has to go to the library, and I go back to daydreaming. Daydreaming falls into a quick nap, and then the quick nap falls into a deep sleep. The deep sleep meant dreaming would occur. I'm in the clouds again, almost identical to my original dream I had a couple days prior, except this time I'm able to move from my position. I float around, until something knocks me clean out of the sky. It felt like something had shot up through my bones and dragged me down with no warning. I slam into the clouds, which are hard as rocks. I slowly start to rise to my feet, but a ripping sensation pulls me back down.

I look at my stomach, and a spear looking figure is piercing right through my abdomen. Everything starts to become blurry. I was flying freely around until I was shot down. The spear is swiftly yanked out of the blue, and I yell in excruciating pain. I sit up, and see a slender figure standing at my feet. He has no mouth, but his eyes and nose is out of proportion, with one eye bulging out of its socket unnaturally. I hear a loud sentence being echoed throughout the atmosphere, and I can make out the words quite clearly, yelling "Become what you need" over and over again. I feel my forehead get hot, and soon I'm swimming in a sea of my own sweat. The man is still staring me down, and I suddenly jolt awake. What happened? I look at my hands, and I see the dried blood on my knuckles. What have I done? I feel like amnesia had just kicked in and I can't even remember where I live. Is this my blood? I'm trying to retrace my steps, until I remember punching the child earlier this morning. I remember the shock of power I felt, the fear on the child's face, the crunch of his nose. I felt like I had a high from violence, and I needed to replicate that sensation again. The clock read 3:45, my detention is over. I stand up from my chair, and marched out the door. I turn the corner to leave the school when I run into the principal and the freshman I beat up earlier.

"Kyle, what are you doing out here?"

I look up and tell him that my detention was over, but he smirks and shakes his head.

"Well, if you would've waited where you should've, you would have been informed that you have an added three hours of detention. James here and many other children told me that you had broken his nose. Is that true?"

I look James dead in the eye. His skin turns a deadly pale, and I could tell he knew what he was in for. He told on me! My philosophy had changed. From not hurting people to beating the crap out of people who get in my way. You know what they say. Snitches get stitches. I launch myself upon James, who shrieks with pure terror. He slams into the ground, and his head bounces off of the tiles. I lift up my fist, and start throwing punches into his head. He's crying out for help, but there was nobody that would dare fight me. I'm landing every punch I send his way, and eventually his arms give out and they stop blocking his face. I'm landing several more shots to the mouth and nose, until I wind up my arm to far. Mr. Haddins grabs my arm and throws me off of James. My back is on the ground, with Mr. Haddins' foot atop my chest.

"Enough is enough, Strong! Instead of having you stay after school longer today, I think a week suspension is an order!"

He pulls me up and leads me outside the door. I look back at James, and he is coughing up the teeth I knocked down his throat. Blood is covering the floor where his head had been, and I laugh. Serves him right for tattling on me. Everyone thought I was I joke, but where am I know? I'm a kid's bane of existence! I'll be theirs too! I'll show them!

I'll show them all!

Chapter Four

The next week was a living hell for James. He would get the exact same treatment every day after school. He'd turn the corner of the school when I would ambush him from behind, knocking him onto the stone sidewalk. He'd look up right before I stomp on his leg repeatedly, each stomp followed by a sharp and short squeal. Each day I would have to wait longer and longer until James turned around the corner. Every day he had showed up with more marks on his body, whether they be black and blue or red and pink. It was becoming the weekend, and on Monday I would go back to school. After school, I would have to go to a conference with the school counselor with my dad awkwardly sitting in the extremely small chairs. I have to make sure that James never messes with me again. He finally turned the corner twenty minutes after the school bell, and I shoved him down onto the ground with full power. He was airborne for a couple feet, and landed with a loud smash!

"So, ready for another round?" I smirk as I see James struggle to get to his feet. He looks up at me, and wipes off his shirt. I start walking over to him, with my fists up, ready to strike. All of a sudden, James pulls up his arm and throws a hook right to my jaw. I hear a cracking noise, and I fall to the pavement. My arm is scraped from the pebbles, but it doesn't compare to the ache in my jawline. I look up at James, and he has already bolted several feet towards the soccer field. My mouth hurts, but I stand up and snap it back into place. I pick up a decent sized rock, and start trailing behind James. He was pretty fast and had a strong punch, but I couldn't even be compared to him. My arms were huge, and my stamina was off the charts. Not to mention I played baseball for seven years, and I knew how to throw. I couldn't run faster than James, and he didn't look like he was even breaking a sweat.

I eventually stopped running, and took aim. He was pretty far away, about several yards. The rock wasn't heavy, but my heart was beating so fast my arms were weak. I closed my right eye, and flung the rock towards James. It was flying for about three seconds before I saw it smash into his head. He crumpled to the ground and didn't get up. I saw him moving, twitching almost, and took the chance to capitalize on him. I sprinted towards him and picked him up. From above my head, I slammed him into the ground. Blood was coming from the back of his head, and I made sure that he remembers who I am. I kneel down and lift up his head with my left hand while I smash his face in with my right. He's looking up into the sky now, not knowing where he is. I can feel my rage getting stronger, and I drop his head. This was for everything I've been screwed over by. My mom, my friends, my principal, all of it.

"Who am I?!?" I yell, loudly.

James doesn't respond.

I pick up his head again, and start throwing punches right into his jaw. His head is bouncing up and down off of the grass, and I'm still knocking him back and forth. I slam his head into the ground one last time, and I stand up. I'm looking over at James' limp body, not moving the smallest muscle. I turn around and start walking home, leaving James to rot.

Chapter Five

"Hey Kyle, it's time to wake up. You're back from your suspension."

I gaze up at my father, who seems to be sober for once in his life.

"Screw it, I'm not going to school today."

My dad sighs, and grabs my foot. He yanks me out of bed, and my head slams into the wall. I fall to the ground, still wrapped up in my blanket. I don't know where I am, but I'm able to collect myself quite quickly. I stand up, but fall down in a matter of seconds. I can't stand upright, and every time I try to, it ends up with me falling once again. My dad is looking at me fumbling and rolling on the ground, not even showing the slightest concern. I finally end up leaning on my bed for balance, and look my dad with anger coursing through my veins. I look outside through the open window frame.

"What are you doing? Get the hell up!" My dad yells, getting red in the face.

I look back at him in the eyes. "Maybe if you didn't beat me up earlier I could get up!"

"What did you just say to me?"

"What, are those old aged ears acting up again? I said if you didn't beat me up I would get up!"

My dad is turning a blood red color in the face, and I can see the rage in his eyes.

"You think you can talk back to me? I am your father! You are my son! You don't have any power over me!"

"In the day I'm your son, at night I'm your punching bag! Pick one!"

"You know I only beat you because I'm drunk! You can't pin that on me!"

"How about you stop drinking then? It's going to your gut, anyway. How about you try a salad once in a while?"

"That does it! If your mother was here, she would have grounded you forever!"

"Well she isn't here, because she killed herself because of you, dirt bag!"

He launches at me, and tackles me to the floor. With about 300 pounds of pressure on my chest, I can barely breathe. I'm looking up to the ceiling, and my dad is maneuvering himself around my body so that he can get leverage against me. I'm able to scream loudly for help, but my dad lifts me up, barely struggling, and launches me onto the floor once again. My head bangs onto the floor with a loud thud and my vision gets blurry. I can my feel my conscience fading away after every punch my Father throws at me.

"You think it's funny to make fun of your father? You were always ungrateful you little brat!"

My dad bashes my face in with one last punch, and leaves the room. My face is bulging, and I can't move. I can only see colors now, and no definite shape is visible. I close my eyes, and I fade off into another dream.

I'm walking back from school, but I'm going at an oddly slow pace, taking about a step every five seconds. I look back, and the sky gets dark. I see a giant cloud swirling into a human shape. It seems to form into someone I recognize. I gasp as I can see the face of James, swollen and bruised. A face that was the size of a building. I chuckle, but James starts following me, vigorously. I can feel the blood drain from my face. I try and bolt away from James, but alas, I am still walking at my slowed pace. I keep looking back, James nearing closer by the second. I close my eyes, and keep telling myself it's just a dream. I hear a loud moan, a moan that could cause an avalanche. I open my eyes again, and James' face slowly starts unhinging its mouth, similar to Ashton and the freshman did in my first dream. I stop moving, and shut my eyes. I'm ready for about anything now, until I jolt awake.

I'm sitting in a hospital bed, my head pounding. I rub my forehead, and I feel a thick layer of gauze wrapped around my head. I look around, and the only things inside the small room is my bed and a nightstand with my cell phone atop of it. The door seems to be locked, as I can see a small padlock on the doorknob, the key hanging on the wall from a hook. I'm trying to remember, but between the numbness in my face and weakness throughout my muscles, I can't seem to focus. I start to fall asleep again, but my phone ringing nearly makes me fall out of my bed. I can't reach my phone without getting up, so the automatic voicemail machine kicks in after a while of ringing.

"Um...hello? Yes, hello. My name is Carter, and I'm with Child Protective Services down here in Detroit. The Novocain should start to wear off in a couple of hours, so I'm not sure if you can hear me or not currently. I've just wanted you to know that you are safe, Mister...Kyle. We have placed your father behind bars, for many offenses such as child abuse and neglect on multiple occasions. A neighbor said they heard a loud scream from your home, 284 Brush Park. They contacted 911, and we found your limp body in a heap on the floor, and your father in the living room. We have also received a report that your father's alcoholism has worsened over the past years, and he has developed alcohol poisoning. If you need anything, just call us back."

I'm still in shock, and I don't know what to think. Is my dad going to be okay? Am I going to be okay? Where's Ashton? I get up, although it's hard it is to move, I start to limp over to the door. I unlock the padlock, throwing it upon my bed along with the key that set me free from my room. Looking outside in the hallway, I slowly but surely make my way to the front desk. The wall contains a huge piece of parchment paper, neatly organized with all of the patients' names in alphabetical order. I drop down to my name, and it reads:

Strong, Kyle. Room 63, Injury Section 2, Conflicts: Head Trauma and bruised body.

I start quickly skimming down the list to compare everyone else's "conflicts" as they called it. Only a couple people seemed severely hurt, which was in a separate section. I quickly glanced at the problems there. It was really bad, with cases such as surgeries and dying people it seemed. One stood out to me, one that was halfway cover up by a flier someone had rudely placed there. From what I could see, it said "cranium and brain damage, permanent." I didn't even want to know who could possibly live through this, but it somehow intrigued me. I lifted up the piece of paper, and the details were revealed:

Fredrickson, James. Room 26, Head Injury Section 4, Cancer Section 2, Conflicts: Fractured Skull

Could that really be James? My James? I did hit him a little too hard, but did I actually fracture his skull? My eyes start to well up. Tears are streaming from my eyes, burning my cheeks. I can't believe what I've done. I slowly walk towards my room again, wanting to die. How could I be such a monster? I open the door to my room, and plop down onto my bed. Everything is hurting, but I can't even focus on the pain. I dig my face down into the hospital pillow, and in a matter of minutes, I'm in the world of dreams once more. Like always, I'm floating through the clouds, not a person in sight. I seem to be very alert in the situation, like I was a marine that is looking for hostile enemies nearby. Soon afterwards, I suddenly slam into a force field of some sort, and I can see the three figures I've seen in previous dreams. Ashton, the freshman, and the boy with no mouth. As the three come into focus, I can make out the face of the freshman.

James.

"Well, it seems you've become what you've needed, Kyle. You needed to become a jerk, a bully, an egotistical maniac that picks on smaller kids. I understand why you did it. You needed to get rid of all that build up anger. From your dads beating to your mom's unpredictable suicide, you needed to take your anger out on someone. You could only get back at your crappy lifestyle by making someone else's even worse. A cancer patient, well that's a little far. You have no friends anymore, nobody to trust, nobody to help you, nobody to care about you. Nobody wants that, but if you do, that's great. Don't plan on having anybody to talk to with. Don't plan on having anyone to play with. Don't even plan on having your parents support on anything you do. But, congratulations, you've officially done it. Well done, Kyle."

I'm slipping out of my dream, and I'm screaming at the top of my lungs. I need to make things right with these three, but how? They're only accessible in my imagination. I'm pleading and begging them to keep me asleep, but they show not even the slightest amount of ambition to help. James looks up at me one more time.

"Well done."

Forgiveness Is A Great Thing, But Kindness Is Golden!

By: Molly Braskich

It is crazy how one person can change your life in so many ways. How guilt can eat away at you for as long as it wants. How easy it is to say something and mean a completely different thing. Let's just say, a lot of crazy things happened to me last year.

Her name was Luna. A perfect, lovely sounding name. A name that I was jealous of. A name better than mine. Everything about her was better than me. Before I met her, I was the perfect student and the most trusted friend. Somehow after I met her, that all changed.

On the first day of school I had my favorite things all ready to go: Vera Bradley backpack, American eagle shirt, Converse shoes, and all of my friends. We walked into class and there was Luna, the new kid, sitting at her desk ready to go and ruin my life. I walked up to her and introduced myself. We talked for a while and became friends quickly. I invited her to sit with us at lunch and the school day started.

I got to know Luna more and more and after a while we had our first sleepover and we grew closer. After a few months things started to get shaky between us because I was jealous. Luna started making more friends than even me, and her social status was slowly rising above mine. How was that possible? I knew that could not happen. I also knew I had to be the one to stop her. It wouldn't take much because I learned that she is pretty sensitive. I created a group text on my phone -not including Luna- and just stretched the truth a little bit. I told everyone something about Luna that might make her not have as many friends. I figured they would let it be, drift away from her, and everything would be ok. Let's just say everything did not end up ok....

The day after I sent the group text my friends started to drift away from ME and attached onto Luna even more. I could tell Luna was really hurt and the evil me just grinned. I decided to just tell another little lie to make them actually like me and not so much for Ms. Luna. Take 2 on the text message and people actually responded back. But not in the way I expected. The retorted, telling me what I said wasn't ok and a bunch of other adult like things. So now I didn't really have many friends. I was so selfish and all I wanted was my friends back, and I really needed to apologize to Luna. I decided the only way to fix this was to apologize to Luna, and either way nobody had to be friends with me, but I had let so many people down, it was too much to bear.

The day had come. The guilt has been eating away at me all day. I went up to her and at first she was super quiet and didn't say anything at all. When I finished apologizing she was very quiet for a moment. Then guess what? She forgave me.

Maybe Luna wasn't that bad. She taught me a bunch and made me realize that forgiveness is always an option. Even though I was mean, she still forgave me. She didn't have to forgive me, she chose to. It also means that if you hurt someone physically or emotionally, they don't have to forgive you. If you ever meet someone like Luna, you will understand. Forgiveness is a great thing, but kindness is golden!

"To the world you are one person, to one person you are the world"

By: Cynthia Milone

Bullying knows no boundaries. In fact, bullies come in all shapes and sizes. You can't necessarily look at a person and say he or she is a bully or not, because bullying comes from within. I should know because I, Cindy, was a bully. It is not what you think. I never intimidated or harassed anybody else. I bullied myself every time I looked at myself in the mirror. *I have too many freckles, my hair is too dark, I am too fat or too skinny* were just some of the phrases I would say to myself when I saw my reflection. In addition, other phrases out of my mouth were *if only I could have her hair, her eyes, etc. then I would be the happiest girl in the world.* The "her" I was referring to was my twin sister, Elizabeth.

Growing up my twin and I were inseparable. Even though we are fraternal twins, my Mom dressed us the same, gave us the same dolls and toys. One of the many special things about growing up as a twin was getting to start and experience life at the same time as my sister. As fraternal twins, we were never mistaken for one another. In fact, there are times when we couldn't be more opposite. Physically, having different hair and eye colors, automatically differentiated us from one another. In fact, many people used to think we were lying when we claimed that we were twins. Elizabeth always had the physical features that I wanted such as her blonde hair and her deep blue eyes. I always dreamed that I could look more like her. It was hard to branch out and develop our own self-image and identity since our teachers would always compare us to one another. I would often hear, "Elizabeth did much better on her paper so Cindy you need to improve on your overall effort." Statements like these became a part of my own self-reflection.

As my twin sister and I went to high school we started to branch out and develop new friendships outside of each other. Unfortunately, since I had a low self-esteem, I chose friends on more superficial levels, which lead me down a dark path. Before long, shame was a blanket smothering every breath. Often times I would mask feelings of being flawed or undesirable by acting like I didn't care. I did. However, the one person who was not buying my newfound attitude was my twin sister. Her twin vibe allowed her to feel my pain and she became very protective of me. She was the one light in my darkness. No matter what negative things I would say about myself, she would come back with a positive. She was relentless and never gave up on me even though there were times I gave up myself. Elizabeth, my twin sister is the one person who is My World.

Chapter Two

Bystander's Perspective

Broken

By: Ashley DeLuga

Jeffery. Ugh Jeffery. Everyone hated his guts. He bullies Mike everyday thinking he's the coolest kids in the grade but, just because 10 people think that doesn't mean it's true. The 10 people I'm referring to is his "squad" they supposedly run the school and bully the people they don't like. They aren't bad people, expect for Jeffery, everyone else is super nice when he isn't around but, when he is, they become one of him. Jeffery and I used to be best friends that changed in 4th grade. He would barely talk to me, let alone acknowledge I was there. Now, it's the last day of summer and I have to go watch him hurt helpless kids tomorrow. Everyone says 6th grade is easy, and the education is just a joke but, Mike and I beg to differ. You see we're not the smartest kids, we have more street smarts than anything else. We both have an aid with us in very class to help us with quizzes, tests, and homework. That's what makes us even more of targets. We both only have about 2-3 real friends, that aren't embarrassed to be around us, but that's about it.

August 16- The First Day of School

My stomach hurts, I have a headache, I feel like I'm going to throw up. I. Don't. Want. To. Go. But, my mom is making me. That's the text that Mike sent me this morning. I felt so bad, no one ever really bullies me but, Mike is like a human bully magnet. It's bad, and I always want to help but, I feel like I'll get bullied and I like how it is right now.

I get off the bus and as if right on cue, I see Mike get shoved down.

"Ha-ha! The Idiot didn't learn anything about what happens EVERY year!" Jeffery said.

"I….. I…. At least….."

"He can't even speak!"

Ugh. I felt like a terrible friend but, everyone would make fun of me. I just turned around and walked into a death chamber with my head down.

"Hey Mike how was your morning??"

"Terrible I couldn't even bring myself to say anything back to him."

"Oh, I'm sorry, how about you make up a whole bunch of comebacks after school, write them down. Then you always have something to say."

"Nah. It wouldn't work. You know I saw you witnessing them bullying me, why didn't you step in and help me?"

Uh-oh, the question I was dreading.

"Oh…..Ummm…….Because……. Uh…. Look Mike I hate seeing this happen to you as much as you hate it happening, I always want to step in but, I never can. I think it's because I don't want to get bullied. I mean things are going pretty good for me right now and I don't want that to change."

"So your 'track record' is more important than our friendship!"

"Mike, it is not-"

"No, I get it. You don't want to stand up for me because you are on the verge of breaking out of the title we have been held to since the day people saw us. I really thought that you were my friend but, backing out on me like this is… words can't explain what I'm feeling right now. UGH. MAYBE I SHOULD JUST DIE!"

"Mike don't say that. You know that I love our friendship but, I just seem to never be able to help. It's a weird thing."

Yeah, a weird thing called a one-sided friendship. Goodbye Emma."

I never thought those would be the last words I hear come from Mike's mouth that day. I can't believe I let him do that. Most importantly I can't believe that I didn't do anything about it. He was my best friend and I just let him out of my grasp just like that. For a stupid thing, nobody ever talks to me anyway. What was I thinking!

Dear Journal,

Today sucked. I didn't stand up for Mike again… surprise, surprise and now he hates my guts and I'm afraid that he will actually kill himself because of me and wanting to be normal. UGH! Why am I such a bad person? You know what tomorrow I'm going to stand up for Mike, then maybe he'll realize how important our friendship really is to me! Yes!

Love, Emma

August 17- The Second Day of School

Today is the day. I'm going to get show Mike how much he means to me. Here goes nothing. I walk off the bus and see Mike knocked down, I walk over preparing for war. Right about as I get there I see another girl already helping him up and make Jeffery and his squad leave. They start walking together and I feel my heart drop a little bit. I've never told anyone this but, I've always kind of liked Mike and seeing him with her makes me really sad. I walk into the school with my head down, I get to my locker and see Mike and the girl talking at his locker and it hits me again this time Mike sees me and gives me a little glare not big enough for anyone to notice but, small enough for me to notice.

September 17- One Month Later

It's been like that for about a month now but, Mike has never got bullied once, that I've seen, since that day. I wonder what she said, and I wonder what they are.

Dear Journal,

Today was awful not only did I start getting bullied again but, I found out that Mike and Sophia are dating, I have a bad feeling about the whole thing but, I haven't said anything, mostly because there's nobody to tell. I haven't talked to Mike since our "breakup" but, I really miss him. He was always there for me, making me laugh, smile and always sticking up for me no matter what it cost him. I've recently started cutting... again. I don't have any friends and nobody even acknowledges me anymore. It's like they all think I shouldn't be here. I posted a picture of me and my cousin, I got a lot of hate and people telling me that I don't belong here or anywhere. I always just blocked the hateful comments but, it's starting to be too much. The worst part it is... I'm starting to believe them.

With Some Hope, Emma

I went into the death chamber with my head down, as always, I see Mike and Sophia talking and flirting in the hallway on my way to Math, I still can't believe I never stood up for him. Soon enough it was lunch, great just another day I'm going to get a Slurpee to my face.

"Hey, if you think that you and Mike are going to be friends again, think twice because, he hates you and without me he has nobody."

"I realize Sophie, no need to rub in that I'm lonely."

"This isn't about you. Just know that Mike is nobody with me so, it's the perfect time for me to drop him off."

"You can't do that! It's cruel, unfair, ludicrous, he's finally happy and you're just going to drop him off! Not ok!"

"OH, you think you're all big and tough now, don't ya. Well, I'm going to do what I want, and I want to see Mike suffer."

"You know what, I never had a good feeling about you and now, I'm just proving my theory right."

"Yeah, so what are you going to do about, you could tell someone, oh wait? You can't, there's nobody to tell!"

"Well, I could.... I'm going to.... Uh-"

"Exactly, looks like I'm going to need that 2 for 1 deal on slushes now!"

Ugh. She's so annoying, thinking she can do anything she wants. Just like Jeffery. This was probably just a plan so that Jeffery could come up with more bullying situations and comebacks.

September 18- Oh Lord

Dear Journal,

Today during morning announcement Sophia broke up with Mike. He took it HARD. He was balling hi eyes out for a straight 30 minutes, I think he only stopped because, and he ran out of tears. The worst part is he got beaten up at least 4 times in that time period. I would have helped him but, he was in the Boy's bathroom so.

September 23- Here Goes Nothing

Today I'm going to see if Mike wants to be friends again. Here goes nothing. I saw him walk off the bus and get knocked over.

"What are you going to do now? Oh wait, I have an idea, how about you DIE!"

"No, he's not going to do anything but, you are going to walk away unless you want a piece of me."

"Oh, so now you're all tough. Where was that 2 months ago?"

"2 months ago, I made the worst decision of my life, I let down my best friend. And I regret it every day."

"Something wrong here…"

About time the teachers noticed something. Jeez. It's like they're blind.

"Yes, Jeffery has been bullying Mike on Instagram, physically hitting him and telling him to kill himself for the past 3 or 4 months."

"Well then, Jeffery come with me, you are going to become very good friends with everyone in the office."

"Hey, Thanks. That was really nice."

Finally I did something right now, apologize.

"My pleasure and sorry I didn't do it sooner."

"It's cool I'm just glad you finally came around"

"Me too. Friends?"

"Best Friends."

That's the story of how me and my best friend started our wild journey. Here we are 10 years later traveling around the world, telling our story and inspiring kids to do the same. I'm glad I came around eventually to, otherwise I wouldn't be here.

Saving Paige

By: Lauren Myhre

I cried. I could have, I should have done something, anything, but I just stood there and watched. I continued to cry and feel sorry for myself, for Paige. I didn't even know her. People say bullies do what they do because they hate their lives. Vanessa had it easy. She basically lived in a mansion with two loving parents who were never disappointed in her and on top of that, she had beautiful golden hair and hazel eyes and she always walked with her friends down the hall. I always thought Paige was one of them.

I was there, I could have done something. I was in one of the stalls, reading my favorite book when they walked in. They must have thought they were alone or else they wouldn't have done what they did.

"Go die Paige. Nobody wants you here. You and your family always get away with anything and I'm done with it. Don't ever talk to me again." Vanessa snapped. One of her other friends tossed a bottle of pills on the floor in front of Paige. Once they left, I walked out of my stall. I knew Paige was in the one next to mine. I can still remember the sound of her crying. And that was it, I just left. I didn't open her stall and ask if she was okay or get help. I just left. I didn't think she was actually going to do it. But she did.

Paige was gone and it was my fault.

The next day, I walked through school with the feeling of guilt hovering over me. I passed Vanessa and her posy laughing as if nothing had ever happened, as if they didn't tell their "friend" to kill herself. I turned back the other way wanting to say something. I opened my mouth but the words didn't come out. I was still the same weak little girl that let Paige kill herself. I had no idea how I could live with myself. I had to find a way to avenge Paige. This was a task I *had* to complete. I just needed to figure out how.

It was clear to me that it was Vanessa's fault but I just needed to know what they were arguing about.

The next time I saw Vanessa and her petty squad, a courageous wave wiped over me and I decided to act on my plan.

"Hey Vanessa," I said trying to sound strong but it came out close to murmur.

"I'm sorry, you're going to have to speak up," she sweetly replied. I felt sick.

"Never mind," I whispered under my breath. I adjusted the bookmark in my book and cleared my throat. "I know what you did. I know what all of you did." I made sure to make eye contact with all three of the girls. "Well not you, you're new to the group." I saw they had replaced Paige with fresh meat.

"You're going to have to be a little clearer." The girls snickered.

"You're the reason Paige killed herself. You gave her the pills," I accused. Vanessa looked as if she found out the whole world was going to end. Which I guess for her it would.

"You don't know what you're talking about. You're just a sad little wanna be. So before you go out accusing people of these things, know all the facts," she snapped trying to keep hushed.

"What might those facts be? Why did you guys get into a fight?"

Sarah, one of her sidekicks, finally caved, "It was really all Paige's fault."

Vanessa turned to her, "Sarah, we do not talk to peasants!"

"Well her dad shouldn't have fired your mom," Sarah spat. Bingo.

"If you tell anyone, I will ruin you. Don't think for a minute that I won't." It looked like Vanessa was scared and I was the reason. I felt proud. No. Sick. I felt it coming up and ran to the nearest garbage can and let it come.

"Ewe."

"Omg, gross!"

"She just couldn't handle it. I'm just too intimidating." The girls mocked me as I hovered over the garbage can. I knew I couldn't be a victim like Paige, I *had* to fight back. As soon as they left, I busted into a full on sprint, heading to Mrs. Gern's room. I bust open the door and the volume of my voice surprised me.

"Vanessa and her friends are the reason she killed herself!"

"Whoa. Why do you think that?" She said calmly.

"Because I was there. I have her confessing." I handed her my phone with the recording. She played it, remaining calm.

"Thank you. I will make sure that Vanessa and her friends don't try this again." I walked out, more confident than ever. Even though Paige was gone, for the first time, I didn't feel like it was all my fault.

Stand Up For Others and Yourself

By: George Fotos

"Ryan! You're going to be late for school!" Ryan's mother screamed from the kitchen. Upstairs, Ryan quickly shoved his books in his bag and zipped it up. Before exiting his room he screamed, "I'm coming mom!" Ryan swiftly flew down the stairs and out the door into the large minivan. Ryan's mother started the engine and started the drive to school. When his mother slowly came to a stop, Ryan was already opening the door and sprinting to class. Running to first period social studies class, Ryan made it to his seat right as the bell rang. The desk next to him belonged to his best friend, Jeff. Jeff and Ryan had been best pals since kindergarten, and still continued to be for 8 years. As they both got their materials out for history, Jeff started talking. "Dude. Did you hear about what happened to Edward?" Ryan's face stiffened, he was trying to remember who Edward was. "Edward who? I don't know an Edward." Jeff's face exploded with emotion of rage. His hands flew up in agitation, "Edward Jones from the second grade, and his bully, Josh Howard." The air went still, Ryan remembered Edward from second grade, and they were friends! "Oh My Gosh, what happened?" Jeff continued by saying, "Josh cornered him in the hallway, pushed him to the ground, and started saying terrible things to him." Ryan's face went pail, he was terrified of Josh. Jeff was about to speak again, when Mr. Finnegan called him out. "Jeff! Are you willing to tell us what you and Mr. Ryan Sherman were talking about? Or, would you like to get back to the lesson of African Slaves.

Once the bell rang Jeff and Ryan separated and Ryan was off to literature class.

When Ryan was strolling down the hallway he spotted Josh screaming at Edward that he was stupid and had no friends. Ryan wanted to help Edward but didn't want to get bullied. Just as Ryan was about to turn around and walk to class Josh and him made eye contact in a sad way? Anyway Ryan walked away and ignored it. The next day after first period social studies when Ryan was walking to Literature he saw Josh again screaming at Edward. This time without any hesitation Ryan ran back to Mr. Finnegan's class and told him what was happening. Mr. Finnegan caught Josh screaming at Edward. Mr. Finnegan brought all three of them to Mr. Brown's office. Mr. Brown had a few words with Josh, Edward, and Ryan.

When Ryan and Mr. Brown were alone in the principal's office, he told Ryan his punishment. "Now, Ryan. We are very happy for you to have stopped this situation before it got any worse. However, you did know about what was happening to Edward for a few weeks before, correct?" Ryan's face went cold, as a drip of sweat fell down his face. Ryan responded by stuttering, "Yes……….." Mr. Brown shook his head, "Listen Ryan, you need to be able to stand up for yourself and others. You're a strong kid, don't let fear control you. What you did today was the first step in being a strong person, but you do have a two day suspension along with the other boys. We do not allow bullying at this middle school. Is that understood?" Ryan's face relaxed. By the end of Mr. Brown's speech Ryan smiled and said, "Understood." Once they all were released, all three boys met together in the office waiting to get picked up. Josh sat on the end next to Ryan. His face was pale and he held no expression. On the opposite side of Ryan was Edward, hunched over and defeated. Ryan tried to break the silence between them saying, "Uh hey guys so do you want to hang out tomorrow, since we have no school?" Both boys laughed and smiled, both nodding their heads in agreement.

Moral: Stand up for others and yourself.

You Are Not Alone

By: Noah Kyrychenko

It all happened at a quiet middle school in Colorado. Tommy was "the kid." He was extremely loud, noisy and obnoxious. He always got his way and was never held accountable for anything he said or did. There was also Jamie. She was a nice person, always did what she was supposed to do. She was an excellent student who was a highly-gifted listener. Who knew that it would only take one person, Tommy, to ruin her entire middle school career? Tommy was this person. He had always been a bully and these days, Jamie was his favorite victim.

One day I saw Tommy bulling Jamie, whom, I cared very much about. At first, I tried to ignore it because I knew if I stood up for her, the unspeakable would happen to my poor, weak body. I kept telling myself that what I was witnessing between Tommy and Jamie wasn't that serious, but deep down, I knew that wasn't the case at all. I couldn't take it anymore, I had reached my bystander limit, in an instant I went from fearful to fearless. There was no way I would let this happen any longer. That day, I became a man. I stood up for Jamie. I cared more about her than I did about myself. I told Tommy to quit, to stop, to never bully again. And do you know what happened next? Well, with a huge eyes and an open mouth he said.....

"I'm sorry." He said it in an honest and surprisingly polite way. Tommy then proceeded to walk away in an ordinary fashion as if he was too stunned to do anything else.

Crazy right? It happens. It really does. It only takes one person to stand up and make the bully face their bullying behavior. Once someone gains the confidence of standing up to a bully, it is the best feeling imaginable. Remember, you are not alone! You are not invisible!

Chapter Three

Victim's Perspective and Letters to the Victim

Bullying is like smoking, you should never start.

By: Hannah Glazbrook

When I was a freshman, I was the most popular girl in school and had lots of friends, (or so I thought,) but that all changed when I was changing in the locker room. My "friends" were all in the corner while I was still changing because I got out of gym class late. After I finished changing, my "friend" Brie said, "Hey Ella, you're famous!" And then burst out laughing. I was confused and just laughed along, little did I know that later instead of laughing, I would become the thing everyone was laughing at. Not until I got home, I saw the updates of my "friend's" Snapchat story. I looked through all except hers and once I watched it, I was horrified. She had taken a photo of my stomach while I was changing and captioned it, "Who freed sea world?" I was mortified and immediately texted her, "Take that off your story NOW!" "Whoa... Calm down." She replied. "Calm down? You want me to calm down after you compared me to a WHALE?!?" I fumed. "Look, even if I did take it down, it's already out of control on Instagram." She replied. I immediately opened Instagram on my phone and saw that I had been tagged in 120 pictures already. I looked at one on my "friend" Dylan's account that said, "She looks like she only ate hamburgers for the last five years." I reported the photo and moved onto the next photo, on my "friend" Will's account, "Why is there a hippo at Jefferson High?" The photo said. So once again, I reported it, and that's what I did, for the next two hours, cry, report, delete. There were over two thousands of them uploaded in only five hours. Suddenly I heard my door open and my sister Alyssa walked in. "Ella Elizabeth Marks, what are you doing?" She asked, "What's wrong?" "Nothing." I mumbled. "Well obviously there is something wrong," She replied. "Come on, show me what you are crying about." I showed her one of the photos and she gasped, "Oh." "Yeah..." I said. "You need to just ignore it, you're being overdramatic, okay?" She stated, as she walked out of my room. As I got up to close the door she left open, I heard a ding. It was a text message on my phone from a boy named Ryan, "Wow, and didn't know you were so fat." The message had the photo attached to it. Then another text from a girl named Eva, "Why don't you just leave, no one liked you anyways." Then from Oliver, "Worthless piece of trash." The names I got called that night were: ugly, fat, worthless, obese, weirdo, and freak. The next day at school when I sat down at first period someone threw a crumpled up paper at me, it read "Fat girl, just go home, no one likes you, pig." At lunch, instead of facing the cafeteria I sat in the bathroom floor not eating, just crying. I stood up and looked at my stomach in the mirror. *"I really am fat. I'm so worthless."* I thought. After my last class, I started to walk home. "Hey look at the fatty." Oliver who was walking behind me along with Brie. "Wow you're so gross. You're worth nothing you fat sack of trash," She said, "Hey look at me when I'm talking to you." She ran in front of me and knocked my books down and then pushed me over when I went to pick them up. Then Oliver kicked my side, and then Brie kicked me too. They kept kicking me until they kicked my face, and that's where everything went black. When I finally woke up, it was dark out and I could see dried blood on my shirt. I ran home and ran up to my room. Luckily, my family was all at Alyssa's cheer meet. I looked in the mirror and saw that my lip was cut and my nose had bled. I went into the bathroom and cleaned up my face. I decided I wasn't going to school the next day and I pretended to be sick the next morning. My mom didn't buy it and forced me to go. When I got into class, I saw Oliver and Brie pointing and laughing at me. Oliver then wrote something on a piece of paper, crumpled it up, and threw it at me. Before I got a chance to read it, the girl behind me picked it up. Her name was Claire, we didn't ever talk before, but she read it, and got out a pen. She wrote something on the paper. She then handed it to me. The paper said, "Ella is the ~~fattest and ugliest~~ MOST

BEAUTIFUL person in the world." Claire then stood up, walked to the front of the class and yelled, "Excuse me, class, I would just like to say that those of you who think Ella is fat or ugly, are extremely wrong. Ella is beautiful as she is. Brie, Oliver, I don't appreciate you being mean to Ella, she's amazing and does not deserve to be treated like this, and if anyone at this school continues to bully Ella, I will personally walk down to the principal's office and get them expelled." And with that, Claire went back to her seat and sat quietly. I broke down in tears. I would never be able to repay her, as she stopped me from having to live in a world where I didn't know what would go wrong next.

Bullying is like smoking, you should never start.

Dear Victim,

I don't want this to be cheesy so I'll try my best. Remember that others are not really trying to hurt you, they just want to feel better about themselves, which by all means is not an excuse. But don't hate them because that makes you stoop down to their level. Hate doesn't solve any issues. And you're thinking "they don't know what it is like, I have it worse." You are probably right. I have barely ever been bullied. At least to my face. But even when a person says something small that's bad about me, I start to believe it's true. The smallest thing that doesn't matter eats away at me. How stupid is that! I can only imagine what you're going through. But try to rise above and don't listen to them. And remember that it will be over soon. School doesn't last forever and how you are feeling now is only temporary. That doesn't mean every single person will always be nice to you, but just try to. I don't know if this helped at all, but if it did help just one person, that's all I need.

By: Julia Touvannas

Dear Victim,

Sure you might have been bullied and it might hurt a lot, but here are things you should remember to say to yourself when looking into the mirror:

1. YOU ARE AWESOME! Nobody can tell you who you are, only you know that! Never change! Nobody can tell you who or what you can be. Just be you – the best version of you.
2. Don't give them the satisfaction of displeasing you. Know that what you are feeling now is only temporary. Don't allow others to define who you are.
3. ALWAYS BE YOURSELF. It does not matter what they like. It matters about what you like and want to do. Don't think that your life is over because your life has just gotten started. And it's awesome.

So always remember that you are amazing and those bullies can't tell you otherwise.

By: Rohan Vuppala

Dear Victim,

I am sorry that people have been bullying you so often. It's tough dealing with these problems. But there are two things that can happen when you get bullied:

1. Let the bully get to you.
2. Don't let them define who you are.

If I were bullied, I would choose the second option. Don't let the bully get the satisfaction that you are hurt. Just keep on being yourself. This probably won't just help you, but it will help the bully too. Maybe they will realize that what they are doing is wrong. No matter what, if someone tries to hurt you, keep being yourself. We should always celebrate our strengths, even if people don't like them. And if you see someone getting bullied, I hope that you have their back no matter what. I hope you remember this message and that you are awesome.

By: Sohan Vuppala

Do the Right Thing

By: Samantha Keating

It all started on the first day of school. I sat down, eager to see my old friends, and maybe even meet new ones. Our new teacher seemed nice enough, and began calling off names, going by last name order. The girl sitting across from me immediately wanted to be really good friends. I was thrilled because since our names were close, I knew we would most likely be together for most activities. Although I was excited, something seemed a little off about her. I had never met anyone who had acted the way she did when meeting someone for the first time. We didn't even know each other and she asked me right away to be her "best friend". I quickly shrugged off the thought, it probably just means she's the nicest person I've yet to meet!

I came back to school the next day, waiting to talk to my new friend, however I was she was no longer the happy sweet girl I remembered. She looked at me odiously and started demanding for my things. Pencils, note-books, and even my lunch. I wasn't exactly sure what was happening, but for some reason, I was so nervous about losing our "friendship". The next day, she asked for another pencil, my last one, and I said no for once. That was when she stopped just taking things, and started threatening me, with painful words like, "you are a weak and horrible person and I don't want to be around you anymore- unless you do something for me...", "Bring me this candy in your lunch, five mechanical pencils, and then you can always be my friend," followed by "You are a horrible friend and you can't be my friend anymore." When I asked about the deal she had previously proposed, she would say, "Well guess what, I lied and honestly, you don't deserve a second chance." She made me feel as though I was the bully. I had never been bullied before, and didn't think it could happen to me. I wasn't shy and tried to hang out with nice people, but honestly, anyone can be bullied. Without helpful, kind, observant people, I might have never realized that I wasn't a bad person and I didn't deserve to be treated like that. This went on for almost a whole school year, and it may never have stopped if it weren't for bystanders who notices and helped. She told me that this girl had treated her awfully for a long time too, and helped me stick up for myself. I still see people who are bullied by this same girl crying, and try to help them out. If you ever see anyone being bullied, do the right thing and take action. It may not seem like a big deal, but you may even be saving someone's life.

Don't Be Afraid to Tell

By: Eva Krastev

Jamie, Grace, and I were all best friends in second grade. We did every-thing together. Jamie was nice, good natured, and she had glasses, like me. We were both big nerds. Grace was humorous and she had beautiful brown locks and cute freckles. She was the prettiest girl in our grade. She was also a nerd. We loved laughing and talking together. But then Grace moved to a different part of town. She went to a new elementary school. We were all devastated. Soon we forgot about her. We made new memories. Then sixth grade came along. Jamie and I were still in all of the same classes. On the first day we noticed a familiar face in one of our classes. It was a girl that was laughing with some students that we hadn't seen before. Jamie and I caught up to her in the hallway after class. That was a big mistake but we didn't know it at the time.

Jamie placed her hand on the pretty girl's shoulder. She turned around. "Jamie? Lilly?" she said. "Hi," I said. *Come on!* I thought. *After all this time, all you can say is "hi"?* "I've missed you two so much!" Grace exclaimed. Then the bell rang and a stampede of eighth graders started pouring into the hallway. We all ran into our next class just in time. Our teacher came in about two seconds later. "Hello!" She said. "Welcome to your first day of Science!" I was really excited. After all I just met my long lost best friend, and Science is my favorite subject! "Today we will be analyzing element cells on the Periodic Table. Please open your notebooks and be ready to write down everything." I was in the process of writing down my title, Element Analyzation, when I saw something out of the corner of my eye. Grace and another girl were whispering something. They were also pointing at Jamie. *Grace is probably just telling her friend about us.* Then they started pointing at me. *Stop it, I* told myself.

Stop staring and start writing your notes. I started scribbling down every-thing that was on the board. "Well I hope you have been writing down everything," said our teacher, Mrs. Kalinski. "This will all be on the test next week."

"Great," I said to Jamie in the hallway. "It's the first day of school and we already have three tests coming up." But Jamie wasn't paying attention. We had just walked into the lunchroom and an entire table of girls was sniggering and pointing at us. "What are they laughing at us for?" Asked Jamie. "I don't know," I replied. "Just keep walking." We strode over to a table in which a couple of students from our classes were seated at. "Why are they laughing at us?" I asked Darcie. "Haven't you heard?" She in-quired. "That girl with the brown hair and freckles," she said as he pointed at Grace, "spread the rumor that you two are wearing fake glasses to make you look smarter. The whole school knows." I couldn't believe this. Grace had always been kind. But when we were little she was always jealous of our glasses. She would go to school in fake glasses just so she could be like us. "I can't believe it," sighed Jamie. I couldn't either. "How did it spread so quickly?" I asked Darcie. I figured she would know something because af-ter the move she went to the same elementary school as Grace. "Ever since fourth grade, Grace has been the most popular girl at school. I wouldn't be surprised if everyone here already knows her." Replied Darcie through a mouthful of potatoes. Because of all of the madness I had forgotten to eat my lunch. Not that I was hungry. Soon the bell rang, signaling the end of the lunch period. Jamie and I walked to our next class in silence. This was a lot to ponder.

On the next day I met up with Jamie at the bus stop. We climbed into the bus and in our seat. "I didn't think Grace was one to be the stereotypical 'popular girl'," Jamie said. It was the first time we mentioned this since it happened. "I always thought that she was anything but a 'mean girly girl'," I replied. "She seemed so happy at the sight of us," said Jamie in a distant voice. It was as if she were deeply thinking about something. We were silent for a while. Then Jamie said, "Why did she say those things about us. I knew she wanted glasses before but... but," her voice trailed off again. Jamie always liked to deeply contemplate things. Then the bus gave a loud *screech*. We had arrived at school. "I hope everyone has forgotten about what happened yesterday," I said. "There is not much of a chance of that happening," replied Jamie. She was right, there wasn't.

We walked off the bus and reluctantly trudged into the school. Nothing strange happened until lunch. When we strode into the lunchroom into our table from the day before. The girls at Grace's table were waving their phones at us. I asked Darcie what was happening again. "Do you two not have social media?" She asked us. "No," we replied in unison. It was true, we didn't. We didn't have phones either. "Honestly," said Darcie sounding annoyed. "Look," she handed me her phone. Someone had posted an unflattering picture of us that said 'They think they are smart but they are not'. I didn't want to let this get to me but it did. I hated it. I wanted them to take it down. "Please don't tell me the whole school got this," I said to Darcie. "Sorry, but everyone that has a phone has seen this." I was really mad at the person who posted it. No, I wasn't mad, I was furious. "Can I borrow this for a second," I asked Darcie as I pointed at her phone. "Um, sure," she said, but I was already out the door and being closely followed by Jamie.

I stormed into the front office. There were a couple of teachers sitting behind a big desk. I recognized one of them as my math teacher, Mrs. Barrilli. "What are you doing?" Asked Jamie is an alarmed voice. But I wasn't paying attention to her. My face was a deep shade of red. I was fuming. "Where is Principal Derrick?" I asked Mrs. Barrilli. "He is in his office, why?" She asked suspiciously. I didn't answer her. I ambled into Principal Derrick's office. "Hello, Lilly. Oh, and, hello Jamie," he said as we walked into his office. "Hello Principal Derrick," said Jamie. "Is there a reason for this visit?" He questioned. "Yes," I managed to say. My fist was clenched into a ball and my other hand was holding Darcie's phone tightly. After a while Principal Derrick asked, "And what may that be?" I handed him the phone. He seemed to be deeply thinking about it. He scratched his short beard and asked, "Who did this?" And suddenly I connected the dots. "Grace Polinsi," I replied. It sounded more like two sentences than one.

"All right we'll see about this, for now you two should go to your next class," said Principal Derrick. I could tell that he was very mad. Jamie and I went back to the cafeteria just in time to run into Darcie. "Here," I said in a small voice while handing her phone back. "Thanks," she said as she took it. Jamie and I turned around and headed to our next class.

Two days later the entire school was called to a 'no bullying' assembly. I hadn't seen Grace anymore and the whole school had forgotten about the incident. Soon I heard that Grace got a two week detention. I had to admit, I wasn't too mad at this. Jamie and I earned top grades in our classes. We hung out every day after school. Everything was back to normal.

I'm Not Invisible

By: Maddie Parisi

Every morning I wake up scared to go to school. Every day I wake up with bruises everywhere. Never have I woken up with a smile on my face, and it's all because of one person. Brittany. I've never been so terrified of someone in my life.

Beep, beep, beep. My alarm goes off. "30 messages from Brittany." They all say the same thing. "You are invisible, you are nothing." On the bus all I can hear are those words.

"Hey Kelly!" *Oh no it's Brittany.*

"Ummm hi..." She sits right next to me on the bus. No wonder no one believes me about how rude she is to me. Everybody thinks we are friends. Once we get to school I run in and go to my locker. Every morning I lock my emotions in the locker. Shove who I am, inside, and close it. Then at the end of school I easily just unlock it from the inside. But today is different. I did run in to the school I did go to my locker but I didn't shove myself in. Instead I slam my locker and go to class. I got to class and I find my seat. I sit and sit until 8:16 am. Brittany looks at me. She says nothing just glares. I burst into tears and without asking I sprint to the bathroom and literally hide. I go to every class for five minutes then go to the bathroom for the rest of class.

Ring, ring, ring. I look at my phone it's 2:20. I run to my locker and get my stuff then run to the bus. While running someone trips me. I look up and all

I see is red hair and basketball shoes. I obviously know it is Brittany without thinking I yell, "Hey Britany what is that for!" She turns around slowly.

"What?" She answers. I don't answer I run to the bus and hide under a seat in the front. I cry the whole bus ride home. I then run into my room and cry for hours. *I hate school, no one likes me, I'm all alone, and would it make a difference if I wasn't alive?* After those words. I grabbed scissors. I did one cut on my arm. I hid it under my sweatshirt so no one would see it. I just rub the blood off and go to sleep.

I wake up go on the bus and run into school. I saw two new kids at school. There is a girl that looked like me and I think standing next to her is her brother. I walk up to them maybe I could make new friends and have someone to go to with my problems. I introduce myself. "Hi, I'm Kelly." I nervously say.

"Hey, I'm Cara, and this is my twin brother Tyler." *Cara seems super nice. I think I might actually make a friend.*

"Oh nice names! I is wondering well since you guys are new and I don't have many well actually any friends I is wondering if well... never mind." I turn around and walk away. *What is I thinking no one wants to be friends with me?* I then hear a guy say

"Be friends?" I turn around. *Did Tyler just ask me to be friends?*

"Wait what" I ask.

"You want to be friends?" Cara and Tyler exclaim at the same time.

"Of course!" I exclaim back.

"Hey you guys want to come over after school today?" I ask.

"Yeah of course."

The whole school day I'm actually smiling. This is the happiest I've been in years. Ring, ring, ring. I rush to my locker then run and find Cara and Tyler. Turns out they go on the same bus as me now. After the long bus ride to my house we go up into my room. I tell them "I have something really important to tell you and I need you to promise that you won't tell anyone."

"Of course!" They answer.

"Okay so, there's a girl named Brittany. She has red hair, she always wears basketball clothes, and she's super tall. Well I've been bullied by her mentally and physically for 4 years." I just told them something I've never told anybody and now I am freaking out.

"Okay well that seems bad Kelly I think you should tell an adult." Cara says worried.

"No please they'll think I'm crazy... I started cutting myself yesterday." They give me blank stares for about 3 minutes.

"Are you joking? You need to get help! This is super serious!" They both yell.

"No please I promise I'll stop!" But I never did.

Every day I cut more. Every day I went to the office. I never told them the truth. They contacted my parents. They took me to therapy, but nothing has changed. I tell them I'm fine but I'm not. Today I met this one councilor. Mrs. Saab. My first meeting is today. As soon as I walk in and I already feel like I can trust her. She is average height, Brown eyes that twinkle, and brown curly hair.

"Hey I'm Mrs. Saab But you can call me Lexi you must be Kelly."

"Yeah hi..." I respond

"Well nice to meet you! We will get you fixed in no time just one rule in here." Lexi replies

"Yes?" I question

"Always tell me the truth. Oh yeah and also remember you are not invisible." She says with excitement.

This is going to be weird but hopefully she can help me. "Okay well let's get started." Lexi says. "Use three words that you think describe you."

"I'm ugly, mean, and invisible."

"Well one you aren't ugly you are beautiful, two you are not mean you seem like a very sweet young lady, and finally you aren't invisible I can see you everyone can see you. Why do you think so negatively about yourself?"

"Because I've gotten called all of it. Well by one person every day."

"Well one person shouldn't change the way you think about yourself. You are you and you is good enough."

"But it's not."

"Well it is to me and so many other people."

"You truly think that?"

"I truly think that."

"Kelly you are a beautiful, kind, smart child. You are not invisible and from now on think positive about yourself."

"Okay. Thank you." The next day I go to school ignoring Brittany. From now on I believe that I am a beautiful, kind, smart girl who is not in-visible. From now on I will not be the victim, I will not be the bystander, and I will stand up for what's right?

Jealous

By: Mallory Collins, Riley Betz and Ella Knight

Hi! My name is Claire, Claire Wilson. I have a built-in best friend, my twin sister, Ciera Wilson. I am turning 15, in two days, which also happens to be Christmas! I'm in 9th grade, at East Bridge Middle School, in Detroit, Michigan. Every year I have been in the same class with Ciera, but this year we were separated. My friend Jessie Meyers is in my class though. The day before Christmas break, I was running down the hall, back for my book and I ran into Jessie Myers. "Where are you going?" She asked. "To get my book". I kept running and running, and I turned around to look and SMACK!

I ran straight into the biggest bully in the school, Avery Milston. She's tall, brunette, and she literally runs this school. She once made 4 people cry at the same time. She transferred from Tennessee in third grade. "Ouch! Seriously! You're that ugly twin" Avery snarled. It hurt. Ciera had beautiful blonde hair, grown a lot taller than me, and had naturally straight teeth. It was a spot that I hated people for talking about. Everyone was laughing. I looked around for help, but no one I trusted was nearby. I kept my head down and decided to walk instead of run now, as I passed, I heard the taunting from my classmates, whispers all around the hallway, "that's the ugly twin." I found my book and slowly shuffled back to class, with my head low, and I didn't make eye contact with anyone.

"What happened to you?" Jessie said carefully, in class, "I'll tell you later" I grunted. She gave me a sympathetic look and walked back to her desk. I sat through the possibly most boring class in the world, with literally a

90 year old sub. When the bell rang I almost cheered. I rushed outside, but Jessie had caught up with me. "What happened?" She asked. I told her the whole story. At the end I started to cry. "Everyone hates me and I'm so mad." I yelled. I expected her to yell. I expected her to say how much she hated the bully. But instead, she just said, "Oh, well you shouldn't have been sprinting down the hall in the first place!" I glared at her. "You were supposed to be my friend!" I yelled and ran away. I slammed the door as I walked inside my house.

I walked into my house, and my mom was in her office on her computer. I ran up to my room, not wanting to make eye contact with her. When I got to my room, I threw my backpack on the ground and buried my face in my pillow. I cried and cried. "Why did this happen to me?" I mumbled to myself. I pulled out my phone from my backpack to check my texts, there was one from Jessie. "I am so sorry, I didn't mean to offend you. I hope we can be friends again! :)", I smiled and texted back, "It's fine, I was just upset." I heard the front door open, it was Ciera. I heard thumping on the stairs, then a knock on the door. "Come in", I said. She opened the door and rushed to sit next to me, "I'm so sorry, I heard what happened to you at school." "Its fine" I responded. "Also there is something else I need to tell you" she said hesitantly.

"You might want to check the comments on your new Instagram post", she said with a frown. I grabbed my phone as fast as humanly possible. I looked scrolled down to see the new picture I posted of Ciera and I, with a comment from Avery Milston. "Oh no" I thought. "Looks like only one twin got the good looks in the family!, she had commented. I pulled my phone out of the charger and pressed the Instagram button. On one of my favorite pictures, the one of me and Jessie on the beach, somebody had commented, "Why do you even try, when everything will go wrong anyway?" There was another comment. "Yo, ugly twin. You're so ugly your sister doesn't even like you." A thought crossed my mind, "Why am I here?" But then I just tried to make everything go away. I mean who cares they are just jealous, right? I knew that wasn't the truth but it was good enough for me, so I went with it. Or at least I tried too.

I woke up the next morning so tired and I had an empty feeling rush inside of me. I never thought that everyone would hate me but now... "Mom." "What Claire." she called from the kitchen. "Can you drive me to school?" I said. "NO WE HAVE BEEN OVER THIS LAST WEEK! "She yelled. I know I'm not the favorite child and all, but what have I done to deserve that. I ate some breakfast and walked on my way to school, Ciera by my side. I got to school and immediately, one of the girls, Carly, called over to Ciera. "Hey Ciera, did you check your text messages?" Ciera flipped open her phone and saw a text from Carly saying, "Do you want to hang out after school?" She looked at me and gave a sympathetic smile. "You can go. I'll be okay." I said plastering a fake smile on my face. "Thanks Claire! You're the best." I was weaving my way toward Jessie when Avery stepped in front of me. "Hey ugly. What's up?" I stepped to the side and she knocked me over. My books spilled all over the floor. Then I saw Jessie running away. I stood up, and with the help of a sweet girl named Samantha, I picked up my books, and ran after Jessie. I found her in the bathroom, crying. "Jessie, what's wrong?" I asked.

"Go away!" she responded. "What's wrong?" I said once again. She started crying again. "Why are you crying?" I asked. "Look." She said wiping tears on her sleeve. "Avery said if I don't stop being friends with you, she would bully me too!" I stopped dead. I remembered how I had met Jessie. It was in second grade, and she was best friends with a girl named Scarlett. One day, a girl named Gabriella was stealing Scarlett's lunch money. Scarlett was begging tall Jessie for help, but Gabriella was mean. So Jessie ran to me, and we were BFFs ever since. "So are you saying...?" Jessie looked up at me. "Claire, I can't be friends with you anymore." She said. She got up, and walked away.

The rest of the morning was horrible. At lunch I sat alone. Jessie sat with three girls named Allison, Alissa, and Sydney. They were pretty nice. A boy in our grade named Gaston came walking by and coughed, "Ugly Twin." As he passed me. I slammed my head on the table. I heard two pairs of shoes walk up next to me. "Leave me alone Avery." I said. A calm voice whispered, "Don't worry, it's just Melody and London."

I looked up. Melody and London were very pretty, popular, and super nice. Melody had her hair in braids, her blue eyes glowed under the small amount of eye shadow she was wearing. She was wearing a grey hoodie and jean shorts. She sat next to me. "I heard about Avery, and I was wondering if you would be part of my friend group." She smiled. I smiled back. "Yes, I really would." I said. We walked over to her table that included Melody, London, Kendall, Ariella, River, Kamryn and Giselle. I said hi to everyone and sat down. Avery was sitting with her group of five other bullies, Jason, John, Cheyenne, Addyson, and Jana. She walked over to our table.

"Hey Ugly twin, what's up Twirl Girl." She said loudly. She called London twirl girl because when it came to our dance unit (she's a dancer), she twirled very fast and very good. River stood up. "Leave them alone Avery." She said, her jaw was set, her fists were clenched, and her eyes were burning holes into Avery's. "Why should I Rivie Bivie?" Avery smirked. River's little brother called her Rivie Bivie. She hissed through her clenched teeth, "Because I said so." Avery finally realized she had lost the battle. She walked away, back to her table where John was whispering, "What happened? WHAT HAPPENED! Aww c'mon Avery! Tell me now!" Avery glared at him and he shut his mouth.

Next class was Math with the 90 year old sub again. "Hello everyone I'm Mrs. MacAfee, but you can call me Mrs. M okay guys?" She said. In my math class was Jessie, who I ignored all day, London, River, and Cheyenne, who kept staring and scowling at me. At the end of math, London and I walked to literature and language arts, Cheyenne came up behind me and pushed me to the ground. "Ow!" I whispered as, London stood right between me and Cheyenne. "Back off!" London said right to Cheyenne's face, "Oh what are you going to do about it, twirl around me!" She snarled. "Oh I'll show you!" London said with clenched fists, right at that moment Mrs. M walked around the corner. "Girls, girls, what is happening here?" She asked, London unclenched her fists and looked at Mrs. M, "Oh nothing, just a little disagreement." Cheyenne cooed sweetly. "If I see anything like this again someone will be in big trouble!" Mrs. M said. We all nodded silently and went to our class.

Soon we were walking home. I hadn't known this, but River is my neighbor. Unfortunately, so is Avery. So as River and I were walking home, Avery came by and thumped me on the back, sending my books flying into the muddy puddles that dotted the road. River stood up and snatched Avery's arm. Avery stopped. River tightened her grip on Avery. "If I catch you touching or saying mean words to Claire ever again, you will pay!" River hissed at Avery. "Now leave." She said. Avery ran away. We kept walking after I picked up my books when River said, "Just tell me if she bothers you. I'll handle it."

The next day, I was in the girls' bathroom drying my hands, when the stall door opened. It was Avery, "oh no" I thought. I was all alone. Avery slammed me against the wall. I grabbed her by the wrist and said loudly, "Avery! You can't do this." I threw her hand off of me. "I'm tired of you ruining my life! Why do you do this?" I looked straight in Avery's eyes, and saw tears well up. "I-I-I well I'm jealous of you!" She stammered. "Really?" I asked, "Yes, please don't tell anyone!" she responded quickly. "Why are you, jealous of me?" I asked, "Well you have a perfect life, you are pretty, you have a nice friend, a twin sister, and I wanted to be your friend, but I didn't know how", she said staring at her feet. "Oh, I never thought about that", I said, then something I never thought I would do, I did.

"Avery Milston, I would love to be your friend!" I said, not believing the words that just came out of my mouth. "R-r-r-really?" She said in disbelief. "Yes", then I walked out of the bathroom with a new friend, I thought I would never have.

Say Something

By: Gillian Kramer

"Ayla, time to wake up! It's your first day of middle school!" I open my eyes to see my mom looming over me. I get out of bed as slow as a snail and get dressed. I put on a blue and white t shirt and white jean shorts. I walk downstairs to find my mom and dad eating breakfast they both smile at me as I walk by. I pack up my backpack and put on my brand new black and white vans. I love them and I hope other people like them as much as I do. I make oatmeal and sit by my dad.

"Ayla are you excited?" My dad states as he smiles. "Remember, if people are making fun of you again just tell me." He says with a serious expression.

"Dad, I'm fine. I'm older now and I can take them." I say and giggle.

I walk out the door as I wave and head to the bus. Once the bus rolls up I find a seat towards the front of the bus. Something I learned from experience is if you sit in the back the bus driver can't see what the kids do to you. As we roll up to school I see my friend Maggie sitting on a bench crying.

I practically jump off the bus to get to her, but she's gone. I was too late. I try to push her out of my mind and focus on not getting lost in the huge maze I have of a school. I hear the bell ring and all the sixth graders push inside to the main gym. We sit on the bleachers and have our principal Mr. Deiner talk to us about rules and just general things about the school. As soon as he's done we get put into groups with the same first letter of our last name and go find our lockers. On our search I meet a girl named Irene who's pretty sweet but shy. I like her and hope to see her more.

"Hi ay - Ayla!" The boys crack up as they say it. "Ayla where's the papaya at?" Says one boy named Peter.

We finally find our lockers and I'm nowhere near those boys which makes me happy. I'm used to people making fun of me, and I lied to my dad it does bother me. It bothers me a lot. After three tries I get my locker open and start to organize it. Textbooks on the bottom, extra supplies on the top, and coat and backpack on the hanger. I take my binder at and find my first period. I find Maggie in the class and sit down next to her.

"Ayla, I know you are going to ask about me so I'll tell you. Some boys were making fun of my Asian small eyes and you know I can't handle bullies very well so I cried."

I just shook my head stunned and said sorry, I told her what the boys said about my name and it made her feel better she wasn't alone.

Our teacher, Mrs. Penhart strides in and starts telling us we have a report due Friday. It's on who we are and where we come from, she calls it an all about me Project. I'm very excited!

The rest of the week flies by and soon enough it's Friday and I'm sitting next to Maggie in Mrs. Penhart's room.

"Any volunteers that would like to go first?" Mrs. Penhart asks.

I raise my hand and quietly walk up to the front of her room.

"Hello I'm Ayla Kutlowski and this my all about me Project. I say quietly as I take a deep breath. I was adopted from Syria when I was two years old. I now live with my two parents who are polish. We have five glow fish. I like to paint and read and want to be a marine biologist when I grow up. I love traveling and animals and hope to meet my real parents someday. Thank you for listening." I say very proudly as the applause roars.

I walk back to my seat and am very proud with my presentation. Maggie goes next and I can't wait to hear hers. During her presentation Peter taps me on the shoulder and tells me I should go back to Syria and help Isis. Another boy tells me he's telling his mom I'm helping Isis get Information. They all keep talking and spreading rumors until I can't take it. I run out of the room straight to the principals and i hear them yell. Snitch and tattle tale!

After I tell the principal he helps me feel better and he takes care of the mean boys who were bullying me. Turns out they were the same boys bullying Maggie. He tells me the best thing to do in my situation is tell someone, because I'm not alone and I can inspire others to stand up and tell too. So too everyone out there you are not alone and you shouldn't think you are. So tell someone because once you've hit rock bottom the only place you can go is up.

Second Chances

By: Emma Harper

"Why are you talking to her?" Janice questioned, her tone fierce and her face a mask of betrayal.

"W-well, I, And What do you mean?" I meekly replied "I was just being nice, and talking."

Janice shot back, mocking me, "Well, I-I think that she's dumb, come here, I need you opinion." And so I followed like the obedient child I was, hoping not to hurt anyone. But, Janice had other ideas when, I was close enough to her she reached out and, smack! I felt, a sting, small by sharp, "What the heck?" I thought startled, did she just slap me?

One of the things I learned fast after this new Janice appeared was to never disagree, never make her upset or I would face the consequences whether it be a slap, a pinch, or a verbal beating.

Janice had been this great friend, we'd do everything together and go everywhere together. Whenever either of us was struggling with something we helped each other or reassured the other. We agreed about everything and we had all the same friends. Janice was amazing, she was always there for me and I was always there for her. I thought Janice and I would be friends for our whole life.

When she hit me it stung and made a pink mark, but the most hurtful part was what it made me feel. They always say it's the thought that counts and that's the only thing that counted when she hit me. I didn't care that it stung, I only cared that she would do something like that to me.

While we were in the library one day and I'd displeased her by not reading the book she'd suggested for me I got an especially hurtful torment. Janice teased "OMG, I just noticed that your ears are giant, how do you keep your head up all day with that weight?" And with that she burst into laughter making me confirm fears I had about my looks, which I hadn't thought much about until then.

I was still the helpful girl from before though, although now I made have seemed a bit more distant, no one suspected anything. They thought I was the helpful girl and never assumed I would need help. Anyway everyone assumed Janice and I were still the best of friends, and we were; to the rest of the world. One time I tried to tell someone about Janice's nastiness and they wouldn't listen.

We were having a normal conversation when suddenly I mumbled shyly "You know Janice right? Well she sometimes laughs at me and makes unkind jokes aimed in my direction."

The girl laughed and replied "You must mean a different Janice, the one we know is way too sweet to do that."

Instead of pressing harder and telling her she was mistaken I just whispered something similar to "Yeah, you're right, I was kidding."

Then I kind of gave up. I thought I was all alone and that no one cared what I was going through. I didn't try to tell anyone else. I tried to ignore her negative impact and I didn't stick up for myself because I figured she must be having a hard time and that she needed someone to express her feelings to, except instead of venting she took to punishing. I thought I was being a good friend by withstanding her tantrums.

Although I withstood her torments doesn't mean I withstood them well, in fact I began to dread even the sight of her. It got so that I would try to avoid her at all costs. It was unfortunate that we sat at the same lunch table.

I thought I was holding up well but no, she was even affected my health. One day, she sat down next to me at lunch and I just couldn't handle it, I felt the pizza in my stomach rise up into acrid tasting bile and had to run to the bathroom. Although I didn't spill my guts into a toilet I came close. I started to realize how bad my situation really was.

I decided that maybe I would talk to Janice. I thought that I could tell her what she was doing and maybe help her if she had a problem of her own. The next day I came ready to confront her, then, when I started towards her I panicked, I saw her and she looked at me and I knew I couldn't do it, I turned and walked to class feeling like a major disappointment. I didn't know what to do, I wasn't brave enough to face her and nobody else cared or noticed my problem.

I'd assumed that I was alone but I was proved wrong when a few days later my friend Melaka came and talked to me. She said "You've got to stick up for yourself, you can't let people walk all over you." I was stunned for a moment, confused about what she was talking about. Then I realized she'd noticed, she out of all people was my light in the darkness letting me know others cared about me and noticed me. It gave me a sudden burst of bravery.

Maybe that's why I chose to confront Janice the next day. I again tried walking towards her, and she looked straight at me, but this time I didn't turn tail and run, I stared right back, keeping a brave expression while behind my outer shell, I was freaking out, I felt the noises of my classmates fade away as I walked closer across the blacktop. I could her the usually steady rhythm of my heart pounding out of control. I suddenly got tunnel vision and all I could see was my goal, Janice, of only I could make it, if only I wasn't so scared. Finally I made it over to her. Everything was moving in slow-mo., until Janice opened her mouth, then reality rushed in like a tidal wave knocking me off of my feet as I realized what was happening.

Janice started in a teasing tone "Hey, didn't you wear that sweatshirt yesterday?"

I stopped and thought, then shot back another question, "and haven't you heard of laundry detergent?"

"Umm, excuse me? Come here." Janice started her voice full of venom.

"This was the time when I either stood up for myself or was cowed by this girl. This bully, who had made my life miserable. Could I do it? What would I say?" All these thoughts coursed through my head and I knew I at least had to try."

"No, I'm not coming over to you to let you hurt me or make fun of me anymore. I don't want you to keep being so rude, and mean. I need you to pick a path to go down, you can stop being a jerk and I'll at least try to forgive you or you can choose to be a bully and never have my trust or friendship again. The choice is yours." Suddenly the reality of what I'd just done settled in and I felt like laughing out loud, but I also felt a huge sense of anxiety, would Janice try to get revenge on me?

After my mini monologue she was stunned for a minute and I wondered whether I had been to harsh as she stared at me with her mouth hanging open and her eyes wide, she wasn't used to this sudden boldness, my sudden retaliation. Then she did something I wasn't expecting. She turned and ran away. I let her go.

I felt great, the burden Janice carried was gone! Then my happiness came crashing down when I found out that Janice was more of a traitor than I thought. She was apparently "crying" under a tree saying I had used her to make friends and then I'd ditched her. I knew Janice was just trying to get back at me and that her crying was all for show. This was too much, Janice was finally gone but now... now I had to deal with her again and convince everyone I wasn't a huge jerk.

Although I still felt betrayed and conflicted I eventually decided that I needed to give her a second chance to explain herself or at least beg for forgiveness. I talked to her and she apologized profusely saying she still wanted to be my friend. Janice had lied before and I hoped she was telling the truth. I wasn't ready to forgive her but I tried again with her. I never truly forgave her and even now I watch her closely.

Janice is much nicer now, and actually cares about other people's feelings. I hope that I've helped her by giving her a second chance and I think that's what everyone deserves, one more chance to make things right. I'm glad I gave her a chance to show her regret at her awful attitude from those horrible years in both of our lives.

Something I'll Never Forget

By: Grace Trumbull

My name is Karen and this is my experience with physical bullying. Mike and I were both in the musical. He was a lead, but I was in ensemble. He bugged all the girls in school. Mike was outgoing, talkative, and wanted to have a lot of friends. The only problem was… he *never* took no for an answer. He bullied me in front of people, even my *mom*.

One time, he gave me a horse fly pinch. Man those things bruise badly. He had originally asked me to leave the school grounds, walk five blocks, and go get a sandwich. A horse fly pinch is when someone pinches a sensitive area in the skin (normally the inside of the arm). It's not just a pinch though, it's a pinch *and* a twist. They are super painful and leave large and "colorful" bruises. Mike also slapped me once. He wanted the answers to my algebra homework but of course, I said no. He got mad. I put my folder in front of my face because he was invading my personal space bubble. When I pulled it down he slapped me and pushed me against my locker. My "friend" Sofia was there and watched the whole thing happen. When I got home, I told my parents and my dad called the school. The next day, when Sofia and Mike met with the principal, Sofia called it "not a big deal". The principal very immaturely then said "Mike, hit me as hard as you hit Karen" of course Mike didn't slap the principal as hard as he actually did to me. Even though I'm the victim I was never brought in to talk to the principal. The way they punished his actions was by suspending him for two days, not from school but from the after school musical rehearsal. Of course, everyone turned on me saying "Mike would be here if you didn't make such a big deal about it." and "You're jeopardizing the musical, it's all your fault". I'm the one who was slapped! That's physical bullying you, doofus! Is what I would have said but that wouldn't have gone over well. Instead I just ignored them and went on with rehearsals. Once I came home though, I cried to my mom. My dad called his dad and they talked. My dad was firm and strict, he made it clear to Mike's father that his kid needs to stay away from me.

Mike never apologized to me. Quite frankly I never really talked to him ever again.

Even though I don't remember all the details; quite possibly because I don't want to, I will always remember the main events. My friend turned on me, I was slapped, I was bullied, I was hurt. But there is one main point I want to stress. It is never ok to physically bully or harm *anyone*.

Stand Up

By: Sienna Makhouf

Another day of being teased by Natalie. Ever since I moved and had to change schools, a group of about ten girls bullied me at my new school. At my old school, no one was a bully or bullied. But I guess here is different.

"Hey, no life! How are you today?" Natalie said snotty, but then grinned an innocent little grin. She knows it gets on my nerves when she calls me no life. My real name is Livia, like Olivia, but without the O. Today I went the long way to my locker so she couldn't tease me, but I guess she went the same way.

"Hi." I answered back and tried to continue walking, but Natalie stepped in front of me.

"Where are you going?" Natalie said firmly, indicating that this conversation wasn't over.

"I'm heading to my locker so I'm not late for class." I replied meekly.

"Oh! We can escort you there!" Natalie started excitedly, "Right girls."

"Yeah!" All the other girls replied and got in my face.

So they started walking and pushed me along for the ride. Since I took the long way today, I was going to get bullied to my locker even longer than usual.

"OMG Livia, I love your outfit! It's so… stylish! Where on Earth did you get it, Costco?" Natalie joked, though I didn't find it funny.

"Yeah, yeah, and where did you get your backpack, The Children's Place?" Jenny asked me, then laughing hysterically. Jenny was like Natalie's sidekick.

I was close to crying, so I started to walk faster to get away from them.

"Oh, don't be upset no life, we're just giving you our fashion tips." Natalie said as sweet as the sourest lemon in a grocery store. She started running to catch up to me.

"Yeah, we're just giving you our fashion tips." Jenny mimicked, following Natalie.

"But seriously no life, I love your hairstyle today. Did you sleep on it?" At this all the girls burst out laughing.

"Hey Natalie, stop teasing Livia. Your lockers on the other side of the school, so you should start making your way over there." A girl named Sophie said fiercely to Natalie. She wasn't part of Natalie's little army, and was standing up for me!

"Mind your own business, Sophie!" Natalie fired back.

"I am," Sophie said calmly, knowing that was a comeback that Natalie wouldn't respond with.

"Yeah, whatever," Natalie mumbled. She turned and started to walk away, with her group of minions following her.

"Thanks Sophie! You saved me from a horrible walk to my locker," I told Sophie.

"Your welcome. But you have to promise me that if they tease you again you'll stand up for yourself."

"I promise."

So that's how Sophie and I became best friends. Also, since then, I've stood up for myself and others so that they won't have to suffer being bullied. Now Natalie doesn't bully me because I showed her that she wasn't getting to me. If you are getting bullied, stand up for yourself and show you are strong and the bully will stop.

Chapter Four

Inspirational Poems

Just Be You

Sometime we feel we aren't that great
Making us feel like we need to change
Change how we look
Or how we act
But there is nothing that you should do
You should be the same
The same person you have always been
The happy, healthy you
Stay how you are
Be who you have always been
Don't let someone else or even yourself
Put you down
Just be the true you, authentic, real
Because there is no need for lies
If you become someone you were not meant to be
Those around you are without the gift you are
The world will never be the same,
So please remember to just be YOU!

By: Grace McConnell

Let the Light Shine Through

By: Samantha Keating

Give up.
Because humans will not ever
Care for each other.
People will always be
Evil.
No one is
Satisfied.
Be Cruel, angry
Never choose
kindness,
Spread
Hate.
It Will defeat
kindness,
Because
It is a waste.
Bully
Don't
Help out.

Help out
Don't
Bully
It is a waste.
Because
Kindness,
It will defeat
Hate.
Spread
Kindness
Never choose
be cruel, angry
Satisfied.
No one is
Evil.
People will always
Care for each other
Because humans will not ever
Give up.

Sometimes, the world seems dark, but when we view it from a new angle, the good shines through. Now read the poem backwards.

Look Around

I walk to class to start my day.
And I bump into a bully on my way.
"Sorry!" I mumble.
The bully angrily pushes me as I stumble to the ground.
Before I know it a group of kids gather around.
That's when I start to wonder, *will anyone bother to help me?*

-Jannah Sulaiman

Why?

> Why do people push us down?
> And make us feel like nothing
> Why do people pick on us?
> And point out all are flaws
> When this happens
> It breaks our heart into shreds
> When people see this happening
> Will they help us out?
> Or will they just sit and watch
> Why do people do this?
> And make us feel like nothing
> Do they want to knock us down?
> Or make them feel better about themselves
Why can't they just be nice to us?
And let us live our lives as happy as can be.

By: Grace McConnell

You Are Amazing and Beautiful

No, you are not invisible, although you may think so
You are always wanted, although you may not think so
You are beautiful and amazing, although you may not think so
So never let yourself get pushed way down low
Everything about you is important and special,
from your head to your toes

By: Emma Harper

About the Author

"Empower youth and impact the future." Eagles Rise Up, a student leaders club from Lake Zurich Middle School South want to take their readers on a journey. The destination is a place where peers are recognized for their insights and their voices are heard. These young authors consist of 27 students ranging in ages from 11-14. With the support and heart of their teacher, Cynthia Milone, these young authors ring truth on the pages of "You Are Not Invisible."

Made in the USA
Columbia, SC
13 March 2019